HUNTING FOR GAME

MICHAEL KINGSWOOD

Contents

About This Book

From a secluded hunting blind that no one else knows about, a man goes hunting for more than just game.

Hunting For Game is a 2,500 word crime story.

Enjoy the book! After you're done, please come to Michael's website and sign up for his mailing list at michaelkingswood.com/newsletter-signup/. Guaranteed to be spam free, he uses it to announce new releases and special promotions for his fans.

Hunting For Game

George opened up the trunk of his blue Ford Focus and hefted a brown canvas duffle bag out. He shifted his torso, slinging the duffle over his left shoulder, and grunted softly at the weight of the bag's contents. He'd thrown that shoulder out once about five years earlier while weight lifting, and sometimes he had flare-ups from it. He hadn't had one in a while...until just this moment.

Wasn't that just great.

George gritted his teeth and slammed the trunk shut, then hit the key fob to lock the car up and turned away.

He was parked off of a two-lane country road that had departed from the main highway three miles back the way he'd come. The road had twisted and turned through rolling hills covered with lush green forest until he'd reached this spot, and he'd pulled off behind a billboard sign for a roadhouse bar and grill ten miles farther on.

Stepping out from behind the billboard, he glanced left and right; no one was around. That was good. He'd be out in his stand for several hours, probably. It was his secret place, and he didn't want anyone to find where it was, or know that he was even here.

That could be bad, and mess up his afternoon. And more.

He also had three grand in cash stashed in the cardboard box that had ridden in the trunk with the duffle. Better not to risk losing that if someone broke into the car, or stole it.

Hence, the concealed parking job.

He'd been out of the car's air conditioning for less than a minute, but already sweat was beginning to trickle down his back from the mid-summer heat and the humidity that made the air feel thick and smell of moisture. Overhead, puffy white clouds moved briskly across the sky from west to east, in the direction he had to walk, and he watched one go out of sight behind the tress atop the hill he needed to climb.

Then he adjusted the duffle and hurried across to the other side of the road and beneath the forest canopy beyond.

Immediately it became more dim, but it didn't cool at all. If possible it seemed to warm up, actually.

George slowed as soon as he was out of sight of the road, and began ascending the hill, being careful to avoid trip hazards as he scanned the tree trunks for the signs he had left earlier. Where was - ?

There. Carved into a trunk thirty feet to the left. A heart with the letters G + H inside.

He strode over and laid his hand atop the rough bark, trailing his fingers around the carving he had made a week ago. They traced the heart, then brushed past his initial to the H, and there they stopped.

As it always did when he thought about

Heather, his heart wrenched in his chest and he found himself gasping, suddenly breathless.

The image came to him of her, thirteen years old with her dark brown hair tied into two pigtails, dressed in a yellow sun dress and beaming an ear to ear smile on the day he'd taken her to see that movie she'd been asking him about for weeks. Why couldn't he remember its name now? If had been so important to her, and it had only been two years ago. Why - ?

Then he flashed to the last time he'd seen her face, how different it had looked from that happy day, and his gasping breathing became a sob that he had to work to contain.

He leaned forward and pressed forehead against the tree trunk, and forced his emotions down. He drew in a long, deep breath. Held it, and counted to ten.

Then he pushed himself back upright and, wiping his nose with the back of his right hand, he turned back upslope and resumed his trek.

The hill wasn't particularly steep, but it was a long ascent and by the time he reached the crest George was breathing heavily and sweating up a storm. But it wasn't far now, so he pressed on down the back side.

He reached his hide five minutes later.

It had taken him weeks to find this one perfect place, and then more time to get it built. Fifteen feet up the trunk of a towering sycamore, balanced in the gap between the trunk and a branching limb, the hide was a wooden platform large enough for George to lie prone comfortably.

He'd driven planks into the trunk to act as ladder rungs, and he took a moment to re-situate the duffle over both his shoulders, like a pack. Then he boosted himself up into the tree.

Once he was up, George dropped the duffle with a sigh of relief and rolled his shoulders. He was getting too old for this.

But he had to do it, for Heather's sake if nothing else.

She'd begun to come with him on his hunting trips, and had started to appreciate them, before -

Again he flashed to the last time he'd seen her, on the flat stainless steel, covered by a blue sheet that the orderly had pulled back so he could see her face. Bruised, cut, battered. Staring blankly into the bright lights of the ceiling, but not seeing them.

Not seeing anything.

George flopped down onto the wood that he had shaped and sanded, and laid into place here. His rump hit the platform, and he leaning forward, elbows on his knees as he pressed his hands to his eyes, willing himself not to see.

But still the image of his little girl would not go away.

He tried to think of another time, a happier time. But it wouldn't come. In his minds eye, his daughter's dead, lifeless eyes turned toward him, and he heard her voice in his head.

"Why didn't you protect me, daddy?"

George jerked upright, and heard himself scream for a second before he forced himself back to silence.

Don't scare away the game. Though that was extremely unlikely, here. In this place. For this game.

George drew a deep breath, then turned and unzipped the duffle bag. Along with his other gear, he had a gallon jug of water in the bag. He pulled it out and drank deeply.

The water had warmed since he took it out of

his refrigerator two hours earlier, but even still it was cool compared with the heat of the day. The coolness spread down his throat and into his belly, and he let out a long sigh as he set the jug down.

Through a gap in the trees ahead of him, a glint of light drew his attention, and he leaned forward again, squinting. The lake, below and a few hundred yards away from his position, was rippling with waves, and the sunlight glinted at intervals off it.

Smiling thinly, George nodded to himself, then got to work on the rest of his gear.

The rifle was bolt action, chambered in .308 Remington, with a telescopic sight. He'd taken lots of game with it over the years. Lord willing, today would yield even greater results.

He pulled a box of ammo and a bipod mount out of the bag, then set to screwing the mount onto the lug at the bottom of the rifle barrel.

As he worked, his mind wandered back again. But not to the morgue, and Heather.

Three months, later, and sitting down with the detectives and prosecutor assigned the case. They'd caught the guy, had him dead to rights. The prosecutor would seek the death penalty, but probably he'd end up with life without parole. So at least he wouldn't be able to kidnap, rape, and murder any other little girls.

The earlier smile faded into a scowl as George remembered going into the courthouse for the pre-trial hearings. Watching as the defense attorney submitted a motion to dismiss.

And then stunned disbelief when the judge granted it, with prejudice.

George's scowl became a grimace as he set the rifle down, the bipod holding the barrel up off the floor now, and opened up the ammo box. He loaded four rounds into the ammo receiver, then jammed the bolt home, chambering a round. He checked the safety on, then arranged himself into a prone position, rifle butt snug into his right shoulder.

He recalled spending a week in jail. Contempt of court from the protests he'd shouted when the judge dismissed the case.

Seeing the prosecutor after he got out, and learning the perp was the nephew of a State Senator, or something.

He flipped off the dust covers over his sights and pressed his cheek against the stock.

Distant tree trunks and underbrush leaped into view in his eye, slightly blurry. He adjusted the focus ever so slightly, then panned the rifle left and right on the bipod, testing its function.

Smooth and easy.

He'd pressed the prosecutors to try again, maybe in a different venue, a different judge. But dismissing with prejudice meant the case could never be pressed again, period.

He walked out of the prosecutor's office, feeling his entire world crumble apart.

First Jane, four years earlier. Now Heather. Both had been murdered: his wife by cancer, and his girl -

George blinked away tears and focused on the sights as he shifted his aim point toward the break in the trees.

There could be no justice for Jane. But there should have been for Heather. And that had been stolen; from her and from him.

Through the sight, he saw the lake again. The ripples running across its surface were stronger, originating from just to the left of his field of view. Shifting his aim slightly, he saw the boat whose wake had been creating the ripples. It had a white hull and blue bimini above its conning station. It was sleek and lacked any superstructure: a speed boat.

And sure enough, it was pulling a bikini-clad woman behind it, on waterskis.

George wanted to smile at the sight, but he couldn't bring himself to. He shifted further to the left, and the lake's shore sprang into view. Large houses—mansions, practically—lined the water's edge. Some were sided in brick, some in more conventional planks, but all had the look of places that had been built in the last ten years or so. Each had a dock, and was separated from its neighbor by a fence that ran to the waterline.

A few had swimming pools in their yards above the lake, and wasn't that silly. All had meticulously-pruned landscaping, and lawn furniture for entertaining.

The house halfway down the lake's edge toward him had another boat just tying up to the dock. A dark-haired man in a white shirt and tan shorts was just standing from cleating off the boat's lines. The sun reflected off the lenses of his sunglasses quickly as he turned back to the boat and reached out to help its other two passengers out onto the dock.

They were a woman, somewhat plump but tall, almost as tall as the man, in a pink and white sun dress, and a girl; though young woman would be a better term from the growing hips that were plainly visible from the one-piece blue swimsuit she was wearing. She had brown hair, like her mother, and stopped to slip on Daisy Dukes before stepping off the boat.

The trio walked up the dock to a paved patio area a few yards up from the lake's edge, to where a glass-topped patio table surrounded by four white slatted chairs waited for them.

The man and the young lady sat down, and the woman hurried up to the house. She returned a few moments later, carrying a tray with a pitcher filled with a yellowish fluid—lemonade?—and three glasses. Her face was in view now that she was returning, and despite her sunglasses George recognized her with ease.

Judge Madelin Rosenburg.

The woman who had dismissed the case and thrown him in jail. The woman who had denied Heather her justice.

George tracked her as she walked back to the table, keeping his sighting reticle on her the whole way, and licked his lips.

He had been watching her, and her family, for months. Learning her patterns. Searching for an opening. It hadn't been particularly hard to learn about this lake house, when they tended to come here, and for how long. The Judge didn't have any social media accounts, but her sister did.

And so did her daughter.

Between the multitude of postings and check-ins those two had sent out to anyone with the desire and wherewithal to look, he knew where to go.

That just left finding the right place from which to hunt his game. That had really been the long pole. A place that was within the effective range of his rifle, and within his ability to get a hit, and was secluded enough that he could be assured of being able to make an escape.

Truth be told he really didn't care all that much about getting away. If he got caught, so be it. But it would be better to make a clean getaway.

He'd finally found the sycamore, and the gap in the trees that offered precisely the right angle.

Then it was just a matter of waiting for Labor Day on the lake.

He kept tabs on the good Judge in the interim, and went to the range frequently to get his marksmanship up to the best it could be.

Now it was time. The game was in the open, and he had his shot.

Justice for Heather. Finally.

The Judge poured cups for her husband and daughter, then sat down in a chair facing George's position, to her husband's right and opposite her daughter. George could see about two thirds of the judge's head over the daughter's. No problem making that shot.

Flicking the safety off, he lingered there, with his reticle centered on the judge's face.

The temptation to shoot was so strong, he almost did it.

But that would revenge, not justice.

George had thought it through thoroughly, and could not escape that fact. Killing the judge would be satisfying. Deeply satisfying. But it would not be justice.

Justice would be to inflict on her the wounds she had inflicted on him. And leave her without recourse, just as she had left him.

He said a quick prayer, asking God to explain what he was doing to Heather. Then he shifted the reticle from the judge to the back of the daughter's head.

He took a long, slow breath. Held it.

And squeezed the trigger.

Thank you for reading my book. I hope you enjoyed reading it as much as I enjoyed writing it.

Every review helps an author out, so whether you loved this book, hated it, or something in between, please take a minute to tell other readers what you thought. All of the online retailers make it very easy to do, and I would really appreciate it.

Feel free to come say hi at my website or on Facebook. I always enjoy hearing from readers, especially since you all are, collectively, my boss.

I also have a weekly podcast, Story Time With Michael Kingswood, where I read stories and talk through some of the latest goings on in my world. I'd love to see you there.

Thanks again. My best to you and yours.

Warm Regards,
Michael Kingswood

Mailing List

If you enjoyed this book and would like word on new releases and special deals from Michael Kingswood, sign up for his newsletter on his website. Guaranteed to be spam-free, you can opt out at any time. And you can rest assured he will not share your information with anyone, for any reason.

https://michaelkingswood.com/newsletter-signup/

About The Author

Michael Kingswood is 20-year veteran of the US Navy submarine force and a lifelong fan of science fiction and fantasy literature. His work has appeared in numerous collections and anthologies, to include the Fiction River Anthology series from WMG publishing. He holds a bachelors degree in Mechanical Engineering as well as a Master of Engineering Management and a Master of Business Administration. He has four children and currently resides in San Diego.

Find Michael Kingswood online at:

www.michaelkingswood.com

www.facebook.com/michael.kingswood

steemit.com/@michaelkingswood

More Books By Michael Kingswood

Glimmer Vale Chronicles

Glimmer Vale

Out-Dweller

Tollard's Peak

Robbed Blind

Wedding Gifts: A Glimmer Vale Chronicles Story

The Falconer's Stairs

Glimmer Vale Omnibus Edition #1

The Pericles Conspiracy

Passing In The Night

The Pericles Conspiracy

Dawn Of Enlightenment

Masters Of The Sun

Novellas

What Lurks Between

The Necromancer's Lair

The Champion

Veritas Morte

Story Collections

Tales Of Adventure #1

Tales Of Adventure #2

Short Story 10-Pack

A Jar Of Mixed Treats

Short Mystery 10-Pack

Short Fiction

Michael has also published a number of shorter works,
links to which can be found on his website.